For Kendra Morris

[a cup of tea,

in the New York heat,

where the Tanagers flee

to Central Park,

where we'll someday meet]

"And I watched her face as she laughingly
responded to something someone said to her, still keeping
time to the muse. When she smiled one saw the
little girl, one sensed the doomed, still struggling woman
beneath the battered face of the semi-whore."

-James Baldwin [Sonny's Blues]

-brought to my attention, the hunger that lived in Simone- a man can speculate beyond what was known, what else is an imagination for? What was known in Julliard, what was known in Paris, amongst the vivid "Central Park Blues," and the "daddy" she spoke of when she yearned for a bit of sugar in her bowl. It was neither here, nor there, anywhere nor with anyone. A man can rise, find his own way without guidance, without help, that is no myth; I found Simone alone, I found Miller alone.

The muse is most essential, the true life of an artist, of a writer. I can live no longer on my own, I have stopped trying, I have given up the swim against the tide and thrilled at the delight of vicarious nourishment. A detailed session of love making is enough to inspire a story, perhaps a novel, living inside of a woman for days and not allowing her to escape, the Tasmanian devil, until her womb burns insatiably, ferally demands barbarism, bare art upon a torn and tattered canvas, bringing into the shadow, the light and still lying in the dim. Confession; I'd rather be bled dry of all the words of dead poets, drained of all the cocaine, the cannabis, the mescaline that will eventually contribute to my cerebral decay, be left alone, aflame in the deserts of abyss, crying into the wind, my tears falling forwards and flowing backwards back onto my face, sleep in the cold, cold rain, jump a freight train bound for the edge of the earth, than live in the flippancy of a void world, devoid of music, devoid of art, of dreams, literature, of the female anatomy, of the free will to kiss gray clouds and deny sunlight its opportunity- I'd rather die, as Dylan, in my own footsteps.

Every piece of art begins in the mind and once it is put to canvas, only then does it separate from the umbrage of the personal manifold; the Vigneron and his grafted vines before they are put into the soil, the architect and his drafts before the adobe is dried, the engineer and his schematics before a bridge is constructed. All evolve around revolution, an unrelenting, unfettered ascent into a new faculty of time, of change and erratic as opposed to the dense pragmatic aegis which we've labeled civilization. It is practicle to attempt to kill a dream, they are pretentious, a vision whose superimposition belittles what we have become. In our failure to understand such unfamiliar visions, we began to fear them, condemn them, sabotage and maim the narrators, imprison our very ability to evolve and thus history is repeated. We plea for such things as self-reliance, friendship, peace and the grandeur of love, we applaud the arrival of new eras that further benefit humanity as a whole. These eras are brought about by those with visions, unorthodox ideal and they suffer nothing less than persecution by fire before they are brought into the light of our eyes, battered and bruised by the pragmatist's scrutiny.

Down Brentwood street, the darkness settles a bit differently than it does in Chicago, then it does in Memphis, along the horizon of the Sargarsso sea, it chafes away at day as time does the man stricken with cancer. A cancer is in all of us, born into all of us and time is never on our side. There is no such thing as a sole survivor; we all get ours in the end, when that end comes. To live life with vengeance, knowing that the end will come. It is inevitable, yet that one predetermined fate cannot stop us now from living, from refusing to live, the fire burning in the depth of the darkened thickets along the roads we've chose to take- it cannot stop time from taking away from the child, its innocence.

The journey to the end of a night is a long one, a wondrous one but what else has man got to do with his time other than walk to his end? Many have gone to that great unknown and many more will follow. Frost's "road less chosen" eventually meshes with the "road frequenly" chosen and they all lead to an inevitable oviduct outside of this life. We are bound, all alive, human animal, by this commonplace destination, by the touch and coitus to reproduce to futhur the haploid of survival. Alive is alive, the burn is the burn; it is clear that D.H. Lawrence has never known that wild thing he spoke of.

The observer is now without his muse and he dies a slow and agonizing death upon their departure, but nearest to his death, he realizes the last truth he'll ever know- that he could never have been part of the world he observed for so long. He was always meant do die outside of their history.

Condemned to this death, a museless death, I stalk the night and the roads in which I once gave homage to the muses, Leigh & Linotte, and watch their ghosts as they attempt to fuck themselves into existence, their clothes scattered on the roads, bare, Linotte's legs over Leigh's shoulder as he fucks her anally. She bleeds a bright red from her anus, a joyous red sparked by the orgasm, sparked by the puncture of life from the phallus of continuum. He finishes, dresses and implore me to take her home at once. Once she finish dressing, I ask her "Do you like being treated this way?" I lay siege to her as Warhol to Sedgwick and tears run from her face. She is only vunerable during the remnants of the orgasm, of the ever echoeing cry of the whipple-tickle though she's never met the likes of the writer. Sex is Linotte's language, the only she is able to speak, it is her only love and perhaps the only she has ever or will ever love, besides the son whom spawns from sex. She is a whore only to coitus, to the sperm she ingest in every orifice, the spasm of the cervix to absorb the hot bolt shot into her and the men she makes of whiffets once they have offered her the nourishment and sustenance she needs to exist. Her 3 erogenous zones must burn with stimulation else she feels dead, empty, lost in that tunnel of oblivion, the tragic-comedy of Venus before the fall. She lives her life to find a home for what is ephermeral, which is honed and molded into what Fromberg believes to be a machine that isn't always used quite well. Leigh is her latest tool and the tool between his legs is her latest device of titillation as her venus is his latest triumph over womankind. Birds of a feather.

Blue wax bleeding from the trees in surrealism, a man with a notebook and camera, the railroad tracks abandoned in the night, long walks through marshes, dampen and cold, the walk back where arousal warms the chilled limbs of the two. They fall into passion. Leigh strips her roughly, barbarously, as senusuality would drive them from 'birds' to "human beings" with human emotion. They prefer the outer realms, as do the auteur in me, the voyeur with whom they performed. Again they visit a ditch, one of which Linotte had become familiar with years prior with a previous lover. Clothes again are disheveled, articles thrown into the streets and scattered about the ditch. Their moans break the veterbrae of the night wind which carries itself into the dream of the woman individuated, turning it at once, into a night terror. Leigh's feet are bare, digging trenches into the ground with the friction he attempts to create while shoving himself deeper and deeper into Linotte's cadging sheath. Hysteria ails her womb which makes conception, in theory, impossible. Such a tale stain Leigh's mind and his seed pours into the back of her birth canal, pulled into her by simulatenous orgasm & finds not the familiar womb of the woman but the barren landscape where the endometrial lining contracts as a volcano, pulling from all that she collects inside of her, dumping it as the pounding from Leigh's fucking presses her bladder to urinary flow.

Splinter aren't enough to stop their indivisible fusion, twigs wrap themselves into Linotte's long dark hair, the cold mud rubs against their skin yet fails to cool their mood until their possession, the curse they have cast on one another by vision, by intuition, by smell, is expelled by exocersism, the foundering of adultery. Their only pause comes when Linotte feels the rub of a stray cat. Leigh looks around and calls her trumpery, until he too feels the cat, now in my vision, rub against his head. Rudely startled, he reaches for the cat in haste and throws it into the street. The comedy rips through them momentarily, until again, lust shrouds all. Leigh continues his abuse of Linotte's venus. I tell Leigh to cum all over her, to give his seed to my imagination rather her fruitless womb. Bruised and battered ribs prevent such expel; he falls off of her after many attempts of fellatio to again arise his phallus. The cold rushed in on us as I helped to dress them and sort the various tangled apparel. We walk back to the house, all in our underwear, carrying our damp clothing in our hands, sharing cartwrights and our last sips of flattened beer. We kiss our odalisque goodnight and sulk in the fumes of her sweet pheromones down the dark country roads back to Brentwood.

Much must be confessed at the anticipation of penetrating a woman whose flower has escaped the peddle-pull of seduction. Linotte is never so beautiful and vunerable until the moment she is lost in that drunk state of seduction, the state that many never see or earn, that I, the learn'd artist and voyeur, spent 5 long years in doldrum dreaming of seeing. To step into the world of the muse, the circadian rhythm of the muse, is perilous. It would not only require my sacrifice of the fascination that shrouds my true grit, but my very soul. The soiling of the muse is always a touch and go risk, the go between, where she would rise and regret the malice of artistic wiles and flee in terror of hideous man or fall, fall deep into the crevice of the transposed double and lose what little she may be. But reason has never held a candle to lust nor ever has it been in the vicinity of being its equal; both the weak and the strong have known this or painfully learned of it. I refused to name her, less she becomes an individual, and thus begins the fracas of self-preservation, self-assertion, a deep credence of omnipotence that originates from accouchment and leaves the void, abyssal and the miscreant scurries to occupy. A serf to a man's bedroom is her ultimate fate, cold chains that will only leave her wrist in the event of decomposition to skeleton. Invicibility is a myth at its lowest in the annals of self-destruction and in those same pages, absolute confidence is for the amateur, for the inexperience romantic drowning in surrealism. Where peril lies, so does the man awaiting the painful birth or the woman awaiting to endure the trauma of such a birth. Mankind can resist not the temptation, the opportunity of self-destruction. The addict knows that their vice is a hazard to them but that deters not the temptation when vice is at hand, in reach of the quaking, withdrawing fiend. I decide not to ignore Heisenberg, the modus operandi of the voyeur and indulge in what may very well be my own destruction. The world of the muse is not my world, it is a cold world, where only your worth is measured by the physical, the superficial, the shallowness expelled, projected and echoed until it recoches into the abyssal thing that pities only itself.

While all along, I shamble on, not behind the muse but behind the night, into the shadows of trees that stand as titans over manmade roads and defects shown in their architecture by the moon as the candle light to a rotten egg. I cry, not due to despairity or naked fear, but because the sadness of the night, the tragic-comedy of the night summons my tears. Embedded in the man who has lost it all, is the night sky, in the history of the American language, poetry and literature as we know it. Hither hereafter the ideal of existence meets hysteria and ignominy is hailed as the jargon of currency that molds a people once scattered by the ruins of Babel's attempt. There are strangers on trains that ride out lifetimes as gypsies, as rubber tramps on the rails. Three times around a block I circumnavigate, going nowhere as the gumption of a toddler, celebrating with dread the anniversary of a child born stillborn. A few days from now, I'll continue to ail and suffer from a broken heart, a father who'd never been or will never be, a husband who'd never been nor will ever be, the caricature of a fallen patriarch without a namesake. Ravens fly by, littering the sky with an unkindness one should never become acquainted with. Absinthe cannot steal from me the bitter taste of failure nor an overdose of Saccharin. The moon summons the South China Sea as the rain carries in me a night that may never end, darkness that I may never leave. I teeter notebooks of what I once naively believed to be the "redefining of the American novel," resurrect and bury Linotte as Tolstoy did his Anna Karinina; he harbored for Anna what I harbor for Linotte, a hatred, a dispassionate hatred. Her womb is tarnished, aghast with slivers of silver hooks, intoxicated with trauma- deep in the center of her I've laid my seed and she's felt the phallic convulsions along her cervix. Her endometrium is ripped free from her loins, the muse of classicists is lost on route to her vaginal gape and silence falls upon the placenta and our child, the effect of the mutter, the namesake of all legacies, falters midstroke and drowns deep in the fault of labor. She was neither from a dream nor nightmare, only a folie and fanciful child still in search of her innocence snatched from her under the very aura of liberation and she searches frantically in the event that she may grow wings and learn flight. I've kissed all I've loved and sacrificed all I've loved to live a life of resolve, where even in the shroud of rigid ridicule- one could be sure of faithfulness and relinquish at once night terrors that has kept him infantile.

The rain from the night sky divides the terror of oneself, the collective wholeness that has become an abomination upon crepitation. As there are moments in one's life where narration is no longer a capability, there too arrives a silence between the question, contemplation, answer, an intermission to an opera where the maestro relies solely on the spectator's omniscience. There is a balance that exists between sadness and blessedness, love and hate, the believer and the non- this balance alone, one can even come to call, with resolve, religion itself. The cold swallows all balance, all equilibrium in me, engulfs me in the premptory flames, a death in motion that goes unnoticed. I lie on the shoulders of this demise as I write pages in my mind of a novel, perhaps the last I'll ever write, the flora of the man who drowns in his own legacy without the attempt of stroke to remain afloat. Daylight breaks into the window and misses fettered manuscripts, notes on the wall, numbers, letters and correspondence of contacts I will surely never contact again. The cold rolls in and there is no heat to halt its charge, my feet are number, socks with holes in them to invite the cold. Scraps of food from trash cans and leftovers have fed me for the past few months. I find bliss in used books, thrift stores, living vicariously into the life of acquaintances, plundering smaller minds into submission, into subjugation, to emphasize their love for their life and significant other yet unable to stop their knees from getting dirty at the base of my groin, as I pledge utter honesty to the next victim. I am in the utero, nestled comfortably in the paper womb that I have molded from the clays of yesteryears and the possibilities of tomorrows. The fall of humanity will never come- the fall itself depends on our suffering, the plentiful woes that seep from the night and echo into the day, it depends on our consistent pursuit of the smiles and denials, our mock regression back into utero. My lack of dismay reveals my fear of nothing, my expectation of nothing besides the inevitable fall of the race. When you relinquish all that is dear to society, you then relinquish your number as a sheep and turn once into the wolf, the independent thinker, in which all sheep fear. I retreat into the four walls of this room, into the four walls of my mind and seek only inward what most search for in the vastness of the earth.

The rain returned, cold and heavy. I am sitting next to Leigh as Linotte is coddled in his lap, under a blanket, sheltered from the rogue drift that has found its way into the livingroom. I am reading excerts from "The Paper Womb," reading to the two muses, themselves, the mirrors, the identicals and their narcissism. They fall in love with their identity, their central theme and legacies and it becomes an aphrodisiac. Words splattered about, the words of a drunken understudy years ago, forgotten as departed strangers unclaimed begin to fall on deaf ears. I anticipate their magnetism to one another, sit aside, smoke a cartwright and allow their vortex to deepen as a macrocosm within itself. Their wicks burn slowly but surely, down to their groins that now flutter and natter to be touch, to be licked and abused. I feed them fables of their world and it is enough to cause the first to initiate the inevitable dive of pigeons. My lies are like chickens, they fly high but not very far; they hit the ceiling, the bounded firmaments and are beheaded, the corpse falls back to the earth, flailing and no more. They leave their trail of breadcrumbs to the bedrooms. I light a cartwright and head out into the cold rain to gather a poem within my mind, the dying stanzas only saved by my suffering, an ailing heart, my ashes raining from the sky onto Kinsey's five thousand hornets wroth in instinct. Rain erodes the tint molded onto my skin from having to endure the woes of the maddened atmosphere as I stroll gracefully, intercepting the rain onto my coat. The cartwright finally gives out, its cherry extinguished by a waggish drop that escapes manumission. I turn for the front door, finding that my hands were so numb that my nerves failed to feel the turn of the knob. The sounds of moans greet me- they are my invitation, the sweetest of sorts, as I shake off the chill that is slit and sundered by the shut of the door. The bedroom door is wide open, the lights off, but their Caucasoid skin gives out their position, their glow, as they burn bright as laterns in the night while flustered and in coitus. I pull the door shut, sit on the opposite side opposite side as to time both Leigh and Linotte's moments of cumming. It is commonplace; their simulatenous orgasms. Linotte is ailed with the inability to keep quiet when her orgasm is near and it drives Leighs closer in when she whispers softly, winsomely "I'm gonna cum." The room begins to spin, every sense in the body becomes exclusive, sharpened, the pulse rises and the beat of the heart is exemplified drastically. "The Little Death" as the French labeled it is just that, the body exertion to near capacity, teetering on the edge of beri-beri to exploit and inject the whipple tickle. Legs over Leigh's shoulder, being penetrated deeply into her humid sheath, Linotte's joyful cries rise, become songs once heard over the nights of the Sodom & Gommorah, as Leigh's convivial seed finds its way to the urethra. He hustles over her legs, straddles his body over her bare breast, places himself in her mouth. He cums as Linotte sucks every drop available from his phallus.

Moments ensueing the delight of orgasmic visitance, their bonne-bouche devoured, they fall over in fashion- Leigh on his back, Linotte to her stomach, electricity still running through their bodies, diluting by the seconds. They exchange sly digs and memoirs of their past trysts, laughing, intoxicated, still swaying from the trauma of penetration. Soon the curtain will close and the show will be over.

Back at my notes, I take a bite into my memory as Proust into his Madeliene Cake, light an unfinished cartwright from the ashtray and let the demons surfaced through my fingertips. They know no limits when left to their devices, no structure, no subtlety; they realize that once you offer subtlety as a human being, you get the ass end of humanity gone into teeth. I type the night away, dreaming as I do, recreating as I do, a perfect life, flawed only by the breath it must take, the breath of life, the sensations against the phantasy. Dawn breaking, light flows in wonderously, the beloved cloister of Linotte still stains my mind as Leigh's seed stains her throat. Stillness is broken when Linotte wakes and warns of her mum's approach, the unspoken writer who left the vaccum atelier for the muses to create their masterpiece. Their departure varies from warm to formal at times, as though sex itself was not just a sacred act, yet a necessary one, natural as the coming and going in and out of this life. Leigh and I climbed into the truck, lit cartwrights for one another and rode the roads and stillness of dawn back to Brentwood.

Dikes and dieties, Franz Fanon, the "beautyful" ones that has not yet been born; one grows weary of the push and pull of progress and antiquation, the lingering past and encroaching presence folding back onto themselves. I settle for anything peripheral, anything ablaze with no purpose other than the kerosene's wayward spill. Jim Crow's kin are still fighting against the typhoon of diversity, of miscegenation, in the southlands littered with ignorance beyond amnesty. If the world were to end, if humanity was to fall, it would begin here. The sun also rises on the one who can see it, embrace it with a wroth dispassionate of a radical. In the south, a defeat at the hands of the backwards clan is not possible when faced with the intellect that stand on their own two feet. Decadence is forced upon one rather it being single-handedly embraced. I stalked through the night, under the night sky, Orion's Belt lit brightly, pulling my attention away from the howls of coyotes. Manmade creeks, sturdy bridges to hold seldom traffic, trees falling during storms, severing both estate and human life lives in what the short-time residence refer to as the "Boonies." To me- it is the escaped, the solitary one needs when sorting through the sum of one's life, the days lived and those yet to be lived. A poet lost upon his odyssey is a melancholy reality, the sounds of Miles Davis's sadness, the blues that englobe the bluebirds that somehow always find their way to and from the low sitting branches. Pine scents the air, overwhelmingly during the summers. The door to houses are left open, to allow the invasion until the wandering poles of the earth dims and invites the loud ringing of the cricket's song. Walden himself found sanctuary in the retreat from the noise of humanity- and decades later, I have found that same sanctuary, the same peace, blessedness in the Dandelion-hued sky above south Texas.

Novels spill from my mind and I devour more as to attempt to fill the warn hole that is my mind. In the front yard, just before the poles wandered and the night came calling, I was reading Colette when interrupted by the passing of a neighbor's daughter. She had a familiarity to her step, to her pace and walk, to the way she stared downwards as she paced foreward, determined to get to a destination. I was reminded of gray flowers, scarlet roses beating their way from the dense brush, the yellow in her parker coat the matched her innocent. I realized I was watching the image, the aftermath of the bloom. She was a waif, the young girl, when I first encountered her, reading Miller when she use to approach me, her temerity still forming and green. The girl in the yellow parker shys away from shag tobacco, from the urchins that roam even the lonesome roads of the boonies, any and all she does, is allowed to do, involves the very separation from life, from what her hormones daily remind her that she is missing. The fresh smell of the flower between her legs is carried by the breeze-I catch whiff of it and at once, allow her to stray away. Virgins know no compromise but absolution, but utter satisfaction; they know not that life is just and at times, satisifaction is never guaranteed and one must make due. They only know and see the one who has annilihated their hymens and with the flow of blood goes the flow of innocence. I let her read Miller, a collection of writing from writers on the city of Paris, even some of my own unpublished works. She is curious of the darkness, of the twisted desires of humanity. Not having known them herself, she craves the rub, the rough chafe along her skin, an abrasion or two to conjole her a bit farther, a bit closer to that night when she would be surrounded by darkness, naked, being flatbacked by the one who happened to have had the fortune, the words, the persuasion, to open her legs and sleep in her womb. And once it is over, she'll see the colors red and orange much clearer, the kiss much deeper, the touch much sharper and the smile much more devious. She'll hide behind her eyes the rememberance of pleasure and lock herself away in the privacy of her bedroom, hands between her legs, reliving the moment when the moment began to glow with rich epiphany. I think of her often, of her flower often, and the years of deprivation it must have known, the years of joyful noise she sacrificed to await marriage, a feat that few seldom meet; the reality of coitus eventually gets the cream, sweeps its clawed paw onto the thin threads that holds virtue to the flower itself.

One is always stymied by the sur-reality of the foundering wiles abundant in the human condition. Nature aggressively mimics, crustraetians in the great sea of wide waves, cluttering our mark upon the nearest stones, the nearest redwood. The supermarket of human suffering is a shoddy supermarket, where no liege lives, no devotion, only the maudlin sycophants whose skin is burned and scarred beneath the torn moquette. On nights when we'd encounter the morass of lost, the bars are overrun with brouhaha and convivial indifference, we commingled, Miller lights in hand, cartwrights handy for our step out for the "safety meetings." The bartender, Ali, was a native of Willis, a smaller town orbiting Conroe, half-bred Hispanic of only nineteen years of age. She pranced around the bar with the confidence of the mixologist, the confidence of sex, the pheromones that fumed from her limbs and the tips given to her by both men and women were a testament to how the bar makes of such youth, Madonna-whores. A man could never earn more money than a woman as a bartender- a woman is a natural hustler, turning men as whores turn tricks in the streets. When inebriated, the human condition confesses authenticity, the horrid spirit, the true perspective. The bartender is the confidante, the therapist and regular suffer, as all those vunerable and weakened, transferrance, the love, the devotion, the addiction to confession, the priest amidst the dim lights, the halo of cigarette smoke.

It defeats days at home alone, falling gradually into the doldrum of abyss, of lost abyssnia, of nothingness. What bleeds from a man who've lost it all mind, is dreadful, a bartender has to be made of teflar, of indifference. With the tact of a politician, of an actress flawless method, Ali evolved from shynesss into that method actress, if she hadn't went through that level of adaptation, she'd be dragged into a mist. Ali prides herself on her hair, as all women who lack substance and relied solely on exterior presentation. She tettered back and forth in and out of a relationship with the same guy for two years and consistenly joked with close regulars who know her personally, that she'd give them head everyday for a month if they were to buy her an expensive gift. The pandering of skin served her well, serves any woman fit and willing to pander well and it resembled so in her massive tips nightly. Serve a man a dream on a platter and he pays any price for it. In the interest of savoring cash for brew, Leigh retreats into himself, in the instance that what may arise in the place of a miracle would be another tragedy preordained to just destroy him. He shares the circumstances with many who have brought the significant others they have split with, hoping that with a few shots and brews, they may compromise, fall into coitus and fall back into love. Lovers reconcile, the ladies sing sweet hymns, their men adore them, coddle them, rejoice in drunken celebratories. It may be unfortunate that puppy live wears thin after a few weeks of rabbit fucking, that substance has been left neglected. Some men just need a chance- a chance to prove that they aren't the whiffets that their women initially surmised them to be. Beginning with the end in mind is commonplace, especially for the one who has been hurt beyond repair, beyond belief and expectation. There is no making a home with the survivor, with the one who has made surviving their number one instinct. They are lost as human beings, venoumous, fanciful and folie. Abandonment is betrayal, betrayal in itself is warranted if the one that you leave has long been an orphan- they expect it and thus abandonment is a mirage.

"The Bluest Eyes in Texas" is sung in karoke, the Cardigans relived in the small bar outside of the city limits, the night is consumed in sensuality- not a cloud escaped the bedridden condition that we call humanity, the cries of despair fill the air and hangs itself around the neck as a Garotte in the hands of a romantic who has lost the muses of his life, the great love of his life, the savors what little is left- the reverence, the pleasure of impression is idle, lowly and a device of misvalidation. The pre-Oedipal blooms only in the event of trauma of birth, the artist only experiencing this because the common person sees not their coming demise, sees not the orange and blue in the skys, Van Gogh's beautiful terror, the roseate dusk that melts into the horizon. Darkest, illicit demons arise and at once it devours all innocence that may arise, that may appeal- time disallows, life disallows- we are left bare to our folie attempt to regress to the womb. "Glass half empty" notes spill from me as my thoughts spin out of control. I find a rogue cartwright in the middle of an abandoned table, as if a tip for the roaming bartender. I find a piece of fire, place it into my lips, light it, inhale deeply and pull another napkin from my gathered pile and continued scrambling notes. From my peripheral, from my utter surpise, came a grudgingly dress woman. She sat close to me and open a discussion on music. We found the we enjoy some of the same sorts, including literary greats of the past. Her name was Pamela Petty and she was a third grade teacher, originally from Corpus Christi, up for the weekend to visit her best friend; a break, I come to find out, from her husband, who was a man of science, a simple man who lacked emotion, depth, substance. Her skin was pale, hair pitch black and carried beautiful curls that sat marvelously past her shoulders. The black irish in her grew to my attention as I once recalled my lectures in ethnology. I could felt the yearn for the touch, the neglect as her eyes burned me with a sensations one gets when first penetrating a woman he has pursued for years. The deafening music then is drowned out, the move and shift of her lips to allow words to escaped became pronounced, the body language that accompanied, the reaction she anticipated from who she thought now a kindred spirit. Knowledge of literature spilled from us as a fresh waterfall into a contaminated gourge, black springs bloom, leitmotif, the melody that seduces the body comes in narrowcast and burkes us temporarily of the modern-day wear and tear of trumpery. There is much that comes in the rain, rain hides the pain, hides the nature of pain and cleanses only what isn't held tightly in our arms. On such a night, Pamela reminded me of this, of the tragedy that festers, the fractures that turn to breaks when untended. The world speaks to those who are able to listen, not only hear words but to look past the surface and see the truth.

Black spring bloom, Danielle Darrieux in black and white sketched in motion across the screen; cinemages dandle the heart of the aspiring auteur in me, the muses, confederates, the dancers behind the curtain. Contemporaries chase dreams in the fashion seen spluttered across the tele; they've no idea that roses grow from shit as well.

Outside, we wait for dark, and perhaps Beckett's "Godot," searching for bits and pieces of more liberation. –we await for it as the clown, the man that may never come yet it stops us not from searching the night madly for him. Time ticks down to our finale demise, whenever that may come, whenever the door will knock and we'd have no choice but to answer and greet. In the everyday life, we find ourselves laced and restrained in straightjackets, blindfolded and at ease in front of firing squads. An old copy of Proust is the comfort, into nostalgia, into regression, it companies me. I had come many miles from the Midwest to find the peace that could be considered a mirage in a noisy America and my return was one of hesitancy. Walden's Pond, James Lowell's view of the Scarlet Tanager soaks into my phantasy, long inspiring me to escape the metropolitan that gave me earlier inspiration and the foundation of being a writer.

Chicago is a callously intoxicating city, infamous and enchanting. The Sears Tower divides the horizon at sunset and the black waters of Lake Michigan are lit by the gaiety of life that radiates from the Navy Pier. When the sun rises, everywhere in Chicago seems a scene from a surrealistic film, short and novel, flawlessly crestrisen. There is a ray of hope in the eyes of travelers and a consistency amongst the natives- the common denominator amongst those who'd hope to be embraced by the bright lights of the Midwest and those perhaps born to them, in the wonder and amazement of the flow of diversity. A scholar needn't trek the world, all they must do is jump aboard the Metra track. You can find the entire world in Chicago; Israel in Skokie, the West Indies off Cicero, the descent of the Levant and Mezzogiorno off Wabash, the culture of Ethiopia in Evanston. Every St. Patrick's day, in recognition of the exquisite and harsh Irish migration, the river is dyed green for twenty-four hours, where it follows the Mississippi into the swells of the Gulf of Mexico, around Florida and travels north against the mistral of the Atlantic current to Dublin. There is neither shortage of overtures around every corner nor a modicum of patina, decadent, whose superstructure rests on the ashes of a previous city.

There are two Chicagos; the one that exists in the imagination and the one that exists, the one that is idealized and the one that holds the share of flaws that any Metropolis may. And within the metaphysical and esoteric world, these two separate entities run parallel to each other and provide that Chicago is the dream to which the artist illustrates, immortalizes and writers bleed their souls dry for a recognition that is only obtained posthumously. The stride into Chicago's "A-List" is an endless marathon in which participants come from all corners of the world to propagate their names on the marquees of success. It is a dream and a failed pander to say that all make it, when in reality, men abandon their families for hours on end to make ends meet, beautiful and aspiring models descend to common women of ill-repute, which feeds a different monster that is only visible in humanity past dusk. And as the number of these hopeful transients and vagrants grow, the paved road to dreams become impassible, fickle, and a wilderness- this is the world where the writer prosper, where they suffer, where endless pages of adage is filed, stored and buried. Chicago is the birth of a writer's life as Hollywood is their painstaking death. There, one has the opportunity to live up to the title "Starving artist." The world fears the artist and the intellect- it takes only great review in the New York Times for them to rule the world. These individuals who have absorbed and have become privy to the superficial medicine and the arch nemesis of mass advertisement; they have seen what lies beneath the seductive colors of billboards, they have ventured into the mind of self-indulgent men and by no means will it be the end of these fire breathing and storefront preachers, by no means, for they hold the principle of basic man, that is, to sink or swim, in the face of chaos and imminent downfall, it is to become vicious and pull anyone within arm's reach underneath. The entire world is in arm's reach of these men and day to day, they threaten to pull us all under.

In a world where we have grown constipated of value and glamour, the culture of Chicago fails to develop the paralysis that runs in the veins of modern America, it has grown immunity from infection. At the age of seventeen, I penetrated my first lover- it lasted all of three minutes, I was impressed with myself- her not so much. At the age of nineteen, I was engaged to one of the most beautiful and gentle woman named Pashalaina. We existed wholly until the time she left me for Mondavi's California. By the age of 20, I had penetrated my twenty first lover- I guess one would surmise that I made up for lost time. Age twenty-one marked the beginning of a spiritual upheaval, when I first truly realized since I came into adulthood, that I was alone in the world- that phase lasted for three years, accompanied with my first bout with celibacy. It was after the loss of my first love that I fled to the Midwest and into the feigned embrace of university followed by military service. I went to Chicago to find one thing and found many others, found the evolution of diversity, of the stroke of genius that followed the Dutchman's sleigh westward in search of adventure, peril, leisure and fortune. I wandered as those pioneers riding the wave of migration and manifest destiny, inhaling and ingesting all foreign to me, all new to me, dishes, teas, cultural practices, literary names I've yet to hear of, words I'd yet to read. Friendships amalgamate easily, without struggle; one can point a camera in the direction of a stranger and worry neither of their bashfulness nor their militancy to protect their privacy. Losing time was commonplace strolling amongst the many side streets, walking the roads sandwiched by brownstones that outdated the second city itself.

I met Amelia in Skokie. She had a cousin who died of Tay Sachs when she was younger and a great auntie who perished in Spilwe under Hitler's Nazi fief- it was stressful and a haunt for her family whose lineage knew nothing short of sufferance and perhaps endured an elongated sitting Shiva. That was the only way I could identify her eastern-European Jewish origins. Her father held a striking resemblance to the temple of Karnak, a subtle and classic man he was. Her mother was the cliché of a nurturer, adorned with the appropriated mentality of protectionism. It was her mother who provided Amelia with her dream of being an architect. At the peak of adolescence, their family frequented Istanbul and during one sunset, when the smell of the Mediterranean Sea fused with an encroaching wind that was all together European, her mother led her to the rise of a Rembrandt edifice, erected in the 532, the Hagia Sophia. There wasn't a building in Chicago that she was oblivious to, not one's history to which she wasn't privy. Her freshman year, she fell in love with Anais Nin, carried a first edition of "Cities of the Interior" and read to me over lunch between her classes at Northwestern. She'd meet me at my favorite Ethiopian restaurant, Addis Ababa, in Evanston, a smile permanently paced on her face, the smell of Prussian Blue still stained on her hands, an old Nikon which never left its place around her neck. She responds with furor when she spots my arrival- she removes the hat that covers my face, the gray scarf that shrouds my neck and tells me that I am no longer a leper. We'd dine for about forty-five minutes, sipping T'ej, sharing critiques on Andrea Molaioli's "The Girl by the Lake," Wende Caporale's art, Sebastian Mariscal's architecture and she'd tell me of great architects of time's past as Theophil Von Hansen, whose Academy of Art and Reichsrat still stands today in Vienna. Afterwards, we'd walk hand and hand to the world market. Evanston was our city, the city built on the palate of an exquisite idea. When Chicago became a mesh of disproportion, it was our escape, the hidden chateau from the world. Not once did we diminish our friendship- we knew that possibly it would inevitably destroy our villa of solitude. I adored her so. When we would sit out till late evening beyond the parks near Northwestern, I'd place my arm around her as she nestled into my axillary comfort and I'd spend the rest of the night kissing her cheek, her forehead, her neck, smelling the sweet fragrance from her long, brunette hair that curled so wildly as to disappear during the night.

Amelia was a friend that only a true man of romantic could cherish, I would asphyxiate myself twenty times over for her and slip into my crypt gracefully knowing that she would go on living, even in the event of my death. I would sacrifice myself knowing that she would transverse the world, putting the world to rights and in her departure, leave superstructures of immense vision for centuries to come. She was the great and I was the poor relation, as Dickens would put it, that she kept. The nights we didn't spend time together, we were much content on departing and perhaps conjuring what it would be to make love. But we never did. We remained close, as close as any man can to a woman without his biology complicating a union. I was twenty-four, yet it was those days I spent with Amelia that taught me what it was to be a friend, the definition I once believed to be, paled in comparison. The irony is that three days before I met Amelia, I had suffered through losing a friend. When Amelia came along, my heart was put to relief and I saw that the former friend and I were both a nuisance in each other's lives, a necklace of stones. There was no devotion, no sacrifice, no confidence- I see now that the former friend left my life to make room for Amelia, who as sure as you could look upon her and know of her brilliance, was a major portion where I wanted no other to dwell. She protected me-instead of seeing my flaws, she gave the perspective that defects are what makes us unique. She has led me to liberation; she has forced me to accept it. I find myself continually restraining myself from taking her to her dorm and explain with my body exactly what she has done to me since she entered my life- hold her hostage until such time the sensation of an orgasm would evoke the nostalgia of our companionship. It was the greatest challenge of my life to forbid my hands from roaming beneath her clothes, my eyes from seeing the exquisite flesh hidden by it. It maddens me to know that her body was a no-man's land, I knew, as sure as a sunset, that it was beautiful. Her integrity cells ensconced a gentle sentimentality, her creativity dwelt in such spacious haven as to leave no vacancy for hate. Upon my very thought of her beauty, I was then sure why I was so ill-at-ease of myself; I wasn't brought up against the beauty of the world, only the ugliness, I didn't take in the sun the way her soul took it in- I was miserable. Befriending Amelia, I was determined to once again find bliss, rediscover the fatalism I once knew from first nature. I was rekindled with humility. I bought her a diamond ring that glow just as she did in the darkness. My military pay wasn't much but I felt obligated to provide her with the most luxurious diamond I could afford- blood was what I owed her, my soul was what she'd taken in its stead. She has found the person that has taken refuge in the writer, saved the man which the world has never known, the invisible man, unimaginative and insipid. I fight for life now, though my head is nearly submerged in the floods of torment, I fight for life, to be- if I owe Amelia anything, I owe her that much, to go on living, forever strung out by her romance. She read my manuscript "Birth, Death and the Murky Middle," and said she couldn't believe someone like me, "the last great romantic," as she loved to call me, could create such a barbarous and pessimistic character. My quotes on romance drove her into a fury, so much so, she had to finish the bottle of Sangiovese di Romagna to give me her critique, to dilute the smelt of her words. It failed miserably, my skin was set ablaze, my mind riddled and severed nearly beyond repair. She knew the animal in which I described in my manuscript was my past self and she made it clear to me that with all our time together, not even a fraction of such a monster has ever surfaced. Put frankly, "Birth, Death and the Murky Middle," was a spit in the face of everything that we stood for; love, romance, amnesty, devotion. Once I reached base, I scribbled on the cover of the manuscript "discard," tossed it into my sea bag and decided that it would never see the light of mainstream.

Years ago, I tried to imagine the most beautiful woman and Kayla was the trifecta of my imagination, Pashelaina was as soothing as a sculptress who molded clay in such a way where she knew how to touch me, Kyle represented the caricature of potential youth, disproportionate change and adventurous allure as magnetic and beautiful as death- the only woman who could bloom into beautiful from eblouissant. Although it was Pashelaina who sent me into the mist of loss, Sara(h) carried with her a part of me when our friendship finally came to an inevitable end. I have only a few parts of myself left, too few to be scattered. They say we are fortunate to have a hand full of true friends at the end of our lives, Amelia is the second finger and if she is to be the only this life of mine would end just as wonderfully had there had been a hand full. So many nights escaped us, slipped away persistently, without breath and all we could do is rest our wandering spirits wherever the sun set was emanated, praising our highly corrupted and erotic Anais Nin, a woman who lived by the shuffle of her desires as opposed to the cries of the hypocrisy of society. I imagine if we have crossed that barrier of friendship, fate would have stepped in, ushered us to a place familiar only to those who have loved and have been loved and the rest of our life would have been decided, hope would finally have dropped its anchor in the harbor of a dream. Twenty years ago I saw God in a dream; I had been waiting for her.

I've applauded the rise of womankind since suffrage- professionalism is the spearhead of their success; their biology rips through the competition and less inept man, their venus the central theme to the entire world. The woman of America is more powerful than ever; she works, she earns, she nurtures, her sexuality has no strictures and she now knows that she can polish this masculine world with mascara, her paucity, that once lived on their knees to patriarchy, now reign as the caste of an undisputed coexistence in stilettos. Amelia had not evolved as Linotte to the goddess her venus could make her, she merely lived to appreciate, roaming those civil-war circa railways and crumbling edifices in an attempt to recreate the art that has been allowed to falter sense the days of Frank Lloyd Wright, of Gustave Eiffel. The cretins of society have carved out their history. Beneath their acquired mentality, they gave birth to a race of inhuman breed that is immune-compromised to the veridical sense- this race, that sublimates the detrimental, gradually takes on human form, mimic the human emotion and lives beneath the epidermal frame, to the point, that there is an inability to deter the madness they commit and the insanity they speak. They are not bewildered like man would if they are to take on an alter persona, they are not dehumanized by suppressing the true self, they gather the vitality of becoming stronger, replicating as bacteria does in the body and thus comes to the doom of the human race. This beast is the artist, the divagated spirit that has come through the testaments and taken on the form of man. There is a strive to the central theme of humanity. To effectively destroy the inferior races (the artist) to sterilize the sufferers and throw them away like lepers, brand them as counterfeits, to engrave a scientific misinterpretation to gain the belief that race has never changed nor evolved nor the recessive gene of the artist and if this is so, the artist is meant to be ruled, not rule. The free world can never falter under the caste of the artist, for they are their own, isolated, ostracized and misunderstood- it is this impairment that men of medicine and politics use to rein over them. In the 50's, an artist who sketched drawings of skeletons, sexual acts, the world as it is, would be institutionalized in an insane asylum and fall victim to faulty medicine such as lobotomies. No man is born to rule or be ruled- it is the position they choose in life. While some are born aware of their freedom of stricture with infinite freewill, other wear chains because they believe it is the traditional way to live. It is not pre-ordained nor is it destiny. No one is born with an innate sense of docility- society and environment superimposes such caste and majority. But the artist is held in servitude by their art, their way of expression and coping. The truth is that within a painting, a photograph or the novel, lives the entire life of an artist, who they are and where they have gone. These works, once they are exposed to the world, are the only ways to disabuse them, the crimes against them, the assault against their personality. The artist is perhaps born, but the majority is molded by their environment- who they are and the attempt to filter out their liberal visions has thus far been a failure in human history. To destroy the minority is to destroy the sufferer. As long as there lives poverty, there is a writer, as long as there are obstacles built to hinder humanity, there will be artist to challenge such disenfranchisement. Johann Sebastian Bach was born with the ability to hear yet we must only speculate that he cherished sound only after he'd lost his ability to hear the sonata. It is a testament that we must lose to gain, fall to rise, fear to overcome and accept to cope. Be that as it may, Bach suffered the loss of his tympanic functions, the loss of a vital sense had become the supreme terror that he recognized, gathered what courage remained, decked himself in full battle dress and marched out against it- if he had neglected that was within his person, it was sure to annihilate him. Bach could hear things that those who were strangers to the melodious and inherited kindness couldn't, that is the voice of human frailty and true empathy. We, as artist, even those of us who have never known a mother, connect ourselves to the bosom of various dehumanizing entity and it in part, becomes the muse of our aspiration, the song we play through the one MC of the world.

Jupiter sees Chicago from its cosmic seat far into the universe. The night is filled with the conversing of human spirits and the flow of music, smooth jazz that has come into the city when it was a town, made haven and refused to be driven from its roots as quarry from the ground. Philosophy fell from the rooftops, the smell of Irish beer flooded the ambient air and I shambled along as Kerouac and Miller sounded by the splendor of Big Sur. The night is invited, exhumed as a time capsule, embraced in the stratosphere as Dylan Thomas's words may have been before his final drink. Dying chapters make their way into my heart, poetry into my eyes and for the first time in my life, I was at peace with the world, with the metropolitans, the seas pools of human depravity. That was the night I met Mancha, the Mali born, Parisienne raised tribal princess. I saw the entire continent of Africa, the suffering in her eyes, the beauty in her face, a true luminary, the living marvel of marvels- it was in her very beauty which seduced white men to Africa in search of this beauty. As Christopher Columbus was landing on the island of Hispaniola in 1492, African women were being shipped to Europa at a rate of one thousand a year for the purpose of concubinage, perhaps the reason why the monarchy has ruled; the very vision of her royalty was enough to lead one man to disparagement. Her body was every known and adored ethnology of the Dark Continent; her eyes, brown with a hint of green resembled that of a Caucasoid, her skin held the ebony glow of a Mongoloid and the seductive physique of Bantu. Ever since I found a map inside of the first national geographic magazine as a child, I'd always wanted to explore Africa and I knew, one night with her, I could trek the whimsical Serengeti, float over the Skeleton coast of Namibia, find the lost oasis of the Sahara and see the Cape of Good Hope and Robben Island, where Mandela lost twenty seven years of his youth to the apartheid monster. Everything about the way she smiled, the way she moved, glanced at me as I spoke, was magical. Her body was glowing in the dim lights of the bar; her breast met each other and protruded from her top. I loved that. I aspired to that. And as sure as she caught me in the depth of a nocturnal emission, my waylay was detected- and she, not afraid of being who she is, comfortable to know that she could show a soft and feminine side, laid one hand on my chest and assured me that there was no rush, Africa has survived for centuries without disappearing into the sea and when she was ready, and convinced me that I was a suitable, but not quite her equal. She would open her womb and invite me inside of the one place in which I've never gone. She left her number and left me so sexually aroused that I couldn't hold a single thought inside of my mind. Everything I saw that night was in retrospect a representation of sex. I texted her the next day just before she got out of class, in haste to finish a dissertation before she was to return to Paris and confessed my infatuation. With reciprocation, she admitted that she had been thinking of me as well. We made plans to call on each other the coming weekend, this time, in a bar close to the UC campus, where unbeknownst, if we felt that same feeling of sexual anguish and exploration creep into our solar plexus, we would only have to walk two blocks to turn these fantasies into reality. Pillow talk is the most advantageous way of communication- once you have spent all night inside of a woman, once you pull out, it seems her true-self comes out with you, like a menstrual stream.

"I want to get to know you, all of you." She invokes.

Alcohol tends to deduce her French/West African accent and ameliorate her English. I felt as though a meek emissary under her regime, the man to enflame her with the chosen heir to her throne. My intellect had made an impression on her and she enjoyed my social nature, my progression in learning the French language withal. She seduced me with the mystic and dying language or Provencal, even then, I didn't feel that her sycophancy was redundant- I treasured our moments of interaction. It was then that she invited me into her womb. She claimed that she was a bit knackered and wanted to go back to her condo.

"Vous me chassez?'

And with that she led me to her royal quarters. Her roommate was there, watching a film when we entered. From her expression, I could tell she too held Mancha to a reverence and also from this look of grace; she registered a plausible disheveled look when I followed her in. The roommate was the third wheel to this effervescent provocation. We attempt to keep the covers over us while we dove into coitus, as I dove into her venus, but it was without accomplishment. Her body was much more than any great mind could imagine, than any brilliant artist could pencil. She smelled of wild coconut with a taste of Serenata de Amor. The roommate who attempted to be coy and focus on her film, attention was on us. She wasn't repulsed nor jealous once her false pretense had worn away. We put on a film that no director could attempt to recreate- we gave her authenticity. Every once in a while she'd let out an "Dieu" as I fucked the princess harder, from the back, missionary, my hands supporting the back of her thighs, her breast the braille to my blind world. I expelled myself, stood her up, dropped to my knees to perform cunilingus then lifted her onto my shoulder against the wall. I drop her back to her back, again push into her venus and cum eye to eye with her cumming and crying in falsetto, emphasizing her beauty. I later found out, while we sat around chatting, that her roommate, was in fact Mancha's cousin and apart of her retinue, trusted to look after Mancha and a virgin. We were a practical vicarious particle that created her world in which she loved to study, mere puppets for her fledgling depraved amusements. There was something wondrous about her, as is with all virgins, the chafe of innocence which gathers momentum. I wheedle my way into the virgin's bed with the suggestion of the princess the morning after. She takes me into her mouth and I cum in the back of her throat, head to McDonalds down the block for a sausage egg and cheese McGriddle and back to base. There I collect myself; flow through the sweet reminiscence of their bodies under the warm shower heads and slept the day away.

A college campus is a universal representation of what the world should be. The diversity of culture, of curriculum, the transgressions and transformation of the pupil, the transference to the Doctors of Philosophy, the place that defies cheap dialogue and masterpieces are ripped free of the professional critiques and ushered out into the world outside into the hands of the harsher critique. I roamed as a ghost that should have been, throughout the century-old halls, under old decrepid trees on fresh cut lawns overshadowed by bygone architecture. Dead air sometimes allows the leaves of autumn to settle and one can hear the waves beating in heavy onto the rocks miles away from Lake Michigan. I reinvent myself, I become my own genre, devise plans to change my name into what Mancha believed me to be, a reincarnation of a Nineteenth century forgotten poet who committed suicide. The paragraphs that I send to her, she continuously proclaims, is highly reminiscent of the telegraph, the verses in the quarterlies printed by T.S. Eliot, rooms, never my own, but rooms for others to sleep, bare art, bare their souls, their bodies to give to their bare-skinned counterparts. Senses failed to be sense in the word but laxed at the relaxation that a campus tends to offer, the becalming of dismay. Conflicts within the understudy are still present as they are guaranteed to us all in our everyday life on this planet and if the campus is dismissed for what it truly is, those demons spew their impish means meanly about and leave scar tissue on all who are attracted by the façade of charisma. While still roaming, this time in the African-American studies building, I encountered the very caricature of one in the midst of the grapple with self. Adrian was an exquisite and remarkable woman. Provocative was her intellectual vanity, her true opinion of herself was most mortifying than I could have anticipated for such a lady. Her mother was a paralegal at a large law firm of African-American origin and her father, a successful lawyer specifying in corporate law of Caucasian descent. The firm is where her parents met, even when it was taboo for an African-American woman and a white man to marry. Growing up, Adrian spent the majority of her time, by choice, with the black side of her family, discovering her black heritage. The more she learned of them, the more she resented her father, the representation of the white inside of her and the entire Caucasian race. Adrian possessed almost, if no, physical traits of a black woman and if upon seeing her, one could bet their top dollar that she was without mistake a Caucasian woman. When in company of those who didn't quite know her, she made it a point to emphasize that she wasn't white and her friends knew better than to refer to her with white pronouns. It would hurt her so. When in high school, she would get into fights and the insult of "white bitch" always exacerbated the scuffle and hurt her more than the physical clout. The treasurer of the African-American students association, though she'd been there for three years and she believed that her white appearance disqualified her from finally making president. She was refused an NAACP award because, as she so elegantly put it, "violated the pre-requisites" which states she must be of full African-American descent albeit her GPA was the highest. It was her greatest obstacle and she felt bloodied and battered by it thus far in life, to be accepted into a race that told her that her features were much too Caucasian, that her skin was much too fair. She was highly family oriented and wished to have a child of her own, with a black man of course, the only such whose genetics could breed the white that she so hated out of her offspring's heredity. There is nothing crueler in this world than someone who hates themselves; their detriment is truly malicious and highly contagious. There is a heaven and there is a hell, there is real and there is convenient- when you force yourself to believe more than the other invariably, it consumes with an inhuman force. Adrian was the true anima sola, ablaze in the world which was purgatory. To many of her friends, her sufferance was seen as an extreme imposition, in that matter, so did her parents. Her father, being a pragmatist with a sense of decency, did everything he could think of, including bribing her, anything to get her to cease hating him, to redirect her anger towards the vectors which disallowed her progress as a black woman rather towards him for creating offspring with the woman he loved. Everything, every act in her life was in direct reflection of her aim to be accepted for who she truly was, there was no way to misdirect her, no pause for intermittence bereft of civility. She was a battle ax, an edged weapon so sharp that it penetrated any and all. My skin by no means thicker than the average man or my heart much warmer haven than any other reasonable listener. True it is a hard world for a child born of two distinct races- but they alone represent tolerance and the commingling of races. The Nineteenth-century Naturalist Louis Agassiz believed that hybrids were inferior, an opinion perhaps heavily influenced by the bias and the scientific condition of its time. The biracial are minorities of minorities, from resistance, they gather strength, even when they embark on the long and confusing journey of who they are and who they are expected to be and from what race; choosing sides is what truly deters who they are- a gray area between a war of ignorance. And like all means of compromise, they are refuted and both races project upon them the stereotypical flaws in which they've fed into. They bear the brunt of frontal assaults on whom they are. If they shall fail, then they'll inevitable fail again, if they should surrender, they'll wave two white flags in representation of their inability to go on and if they are defeated, they are twice defeated.

Somewhere in Adrian's family dynamic, her behavior was passively condoned. Her family lineage dreamed of dreams in the persistent threat that a child may go astray, the only child. Most parents' natural instincts are to protect a child rather identify a problem within them; this instinct is the reason why many children survive the wilderness of childhood, it is also the reason children carry unfettered depravity into their adult lives. It seems oblivious to them that children too can exhibit cruelty. A child left with nothing but the instinct to survive is a sad example. While some children are at rest, singing to the lemonade springs, others are alone in this world and their elegies don not flow with the win yet fall into the earth, never to be heard again. A child that turns inward on themselves is a child lost to this world- they are privy to only one lesson that life has painfully taught them; to devour or be devoured. Not child is easily condemned, as they have a resiliency to physical recovery-they also possess an atoneable resiliency to spiritual recovery because the gates of hell are closed to them. Innocence, however its value and seduction to the world, smothers the flames of infernal damnation and sutures up the wounds in a life that is only given to us once.

I was by no means a kid who knew absolute fortune in all my childhood. I knew of my biological father but I never had a need for him. For as long as I can remember my mother was in an affair with Lonnie Fisher, a man who too knew misfortune in the civil rights days but neutralized when he was sent to the Marines, into Vietnam, where he returned a two-tour veteran and a war hero. At the age of fifteen, I was taken in by Adolfo Reyes, my high school Army instructor, retired Master Sergeant and Green Beret. He spent the majority of his career fighting the factions of Che Guevara, in all accords, a revolutionary leader he respected but he condoned not his politics. It felt great to be taken in but long before that, I had grown a distaste for a father in general and hence, my determination to start a history of my own. I had the capacity to recognize authority, so rebellion was filtered from my opposition and still today, this reason escapes me. Whatever it is, wherever in my soul it may reside, it runs deep. The name Lovett was married into my family and when my mother divorced, it was strongly suggested that I change my name to "Jordan," my biological dad's last name, as my sister Joanna had. The love for my name was immutable and my vision for a new lineage was unvarying as the way of power and greatness. It was then that I had made the decision to change my name, accept the name of that forgotten French poet that lived and self-murdered two centuries ago. I was the last surviving Lovett and now I am the only de Vogue and if this life is to render me childless, then into the afterlife I shall carry this great name. There is no use in trying to convince the world of your existence, you have to be competent to see the true tragic sense of such bewilderment. We all live for a purpose and no purpose is greater than another. Screaming "I am here, I am alive" falls on the world like a heavy rainstorm and only some eyes can see an S.O.S. signal through the immense showers, few cannot, while many will leave you to drown…mais c'est la vie……

Male wasps are lured by the beauty and perfume of orchids; their seduction allows the cross-pollination of the isolated flowers. To further warrant gene distribution, the Epidendrum of panama imitates milkweed, which is a favored food of the Butterfly. Beauty is deceptive and it carries its many ruses- it certainly knows no failure in its narratives when bringing down a man.

To love a woman is to love life and to hurt one is to give up on life itself. There is never a misadventure when venturing into the life of the woman who has taken interest in you and to the one you've become attracted to. The human cells expand, they take on a bit more oxygen, one feels much taller, the boldness, the fearlessness in emphasized, art and outrage then becomes conflated, the kiss becomes the simplest and the most intricate spiritual contract between man and woman. One must live free of complete and utter human contact for there to exist no possibilities of meeting betrayal, but the journey into a woman, is the greatest that any man can ever or will ever embark on. The only way to truly journey forward, is to give yourself wholly to the idea that at any given moment, we can meet that one person that can change our life that can save us from ourselves.

An actor was far from my credentials- never have I changed my personality to please the taste of a particular woman. I offer only a few gifts to woman, which is culture, intellect, worldly knowledge and a chance to take flight and live, even for a day or week, beyond a life of monotony. I wait only for that one sign, one look of a woman dreaming of what could be done to her in the dark. It is then most exciting to be in the presence of a woman with a sharpened intuition- they can sense your eyes burning through their blouse, your mouth watering from the thought of how they would taste and it flatters to the point of an elongated blush, they know that a man, unless he is a botanist or a retired hobbyist, has no true love for a flower unless it is between a woman's legs, Genus Pendendulum, that one forbidden orchid which drives them all men to insanity and propagates the theory that God is a woman, the one Anais Nin so elegantly referred to as "a woman's little wound." Not all women have developed the subtle and expert ways to handle a man of romance in the bedroom, not all women learn to appreciate his poetic words as he free falls into ecstasy. A woman is the victor of this battle of the sexes, she is the curator, made in the image of God, sent through the temptations to tame man by Chicotte; they fall asleep, satisfied as to being triumphal and while they sleep, they seem so much more beautiful, so much more vulnerable. It takes only a few moments of catlike fondling to satisfy again the animosity her body creates and it is done so in an effort as to not disturb her sleep, but to leave her womb burning and in a state of permanent hysteria. If this is what dying is like, then die I would, resurrect myself and die again. A woman's duality seems to dilute her character and some men never seem reluctant to make of the rebellious mistresses, a wife. In Melanesia, the Trobriand islanders are matrilineal, that is they exist in a social order in which kinship, inheritance and possessions are obtained through the mother's relations. The father of the children live to provide, partially to his children and partially to his sister, working days on end to secure all possible. It is not common that he has dominion over his wife, the wife's brother, the uncle acts as the authority figure in the place of the father and thus his nieces and nephews are the heirs to his possessions. But he has few, for his only worth is to work for his sister, for sex, he is in debt to his wife. This tribal way, which was once termed "savage," recognizes the woman's true worth, that her existence provides eternal existence to man; if this is the definition of a savage society, I shall enact my procrastination to hear the definition of todays. Rapture comes only when a woman refuses to be a child. The majority of my female friends were misadventures into love. Sarah, K.B. Nucci, Danielle, Elise; they were all women imprisoned by their own ways. Who am I to challenge their incarceration? Amelia was a different kind of friend. The atmosphere that always haloed over our heads told me that at any given time, I could have her. Her culture was amongst the strictest on a woman, yet she wasn't a prisoner of the traditional chains. Looks didn't interest her- she had the common sense to know that time disallows the permanence of youth. A personality, devotion, honesty, a lifetime of smiles- these were the things that interested her. Being with her and Evanston convinced me that none of those other women, my "friends" existed. It wasn't until I began compiling notes for my second novel "Leitmotif," that I applied pressure to the wounds inflicted by some of these women, others, I simply had to let go. A friendship is tantamount to a relationship, they are both built on the palate of trust, without it, there are just two people dancing around inevitable failure. We make the greatest mistakes of our lives to pretend or force ourselves to make due with whoever is there. There heart must be salvaged, protected from all the different diagnosis, which is seemingly love. One can take that odyssey into the forbidden at their own peril.

I dated Nucci for a few days. Throughout miscommunication, she failed to disclose her attraction to another man, hence came the shortest relationship of my life. My interest in her sorely lingered, there was an artist inside of her, a splinter of a woman privy to her omnipotence; she was bleeding out but she was not yet bled dry. Kyle followed soon after. She was named after a famous reporter of the past by her mother, who was a lady and liberal in all regards. Kyle was a partial fill for the void created by loneliness in the military context- Nucci provided the other hemisphere. One without the other in my life left me wondrous of why I was still interested in the remaining one. It was an extreme mistake to revel in the past whilst making a future with someone- to do so is but self-destruction. Guilt began to chafe away and I found myself so close to the common man that it sickened me gravely. I walked the streets of Chicago at night as a zombie, a lost vagrant ailing with photophobia. In a bar off of Wabash called the Union, I choose a seat at the bar; handle a shot of Clara Petacci, chasing it with a Heineken as I studied only the signs on the wall meant to boast the bartender's ego and mood. The taste of hops disperses like a flurry of an orgasm on the tongue, the cool and cold every man needs after a long day of discombobulating. Writing notes on napkins, I became nearly aloof in the cloak of darkness in the night, in the bar, my eyes on every small detail that arises in my vision. The pleasure of watching the mechanics of mechanical love, of mechanical poetry, drunken dandles, kisses that land asymmetrically askew of their intended targets. Favor falls on the vice, allows it to flutter free of inhibition, over the threshold of forbidden, taking one from the half step to the full sprint. Bravery reaches new heights, the blunt and the brash triggers secretions and the temerity initiated by female is accepted by the male on his primary purpose. The brighter birds of paradise's dances seduce- it is all a matter of the device of seduction in conjunction with the amount of alcohol. Bright feathers tend to dim once sobriety returns but until such a time, the human condition spins out of control, churns all vices into a morsel of sweetbreads in the various holes in the walls up and down the boulevards.

Upon compiling stacks of napkin notes, a familiar face sat next to me, one that I was no fan of. I frequently encountered Lana all over corps school campus in Great Lakes and overheard many of her conversations, the floating reputations and her growing number of enemies. Lana was from a trailer park in Charleston and she was a classic cliché of how one could leave their destination and carries it with them everywhere they go. The majority of her childhood was spent in foster care after her mother became the victim of a crime of passion with heroin until her father got paroled and began beating her. Lana wasn't a recovering junkie, a gold-digger, nor was she a con-artist; she was a manipulator. It is the role that most women who'd been battered for so long assume- they expect to be hit. She loved the melodramatic, instigated and exacerbated any situation whenever given the opportunity. She wasn't happy unless she could spread the detriment in which she herself had endured. It is possible that Lana was born with the innocence that all children possess from birth, but as many abused grow damply, they began to identify with the aggressor; they feel that if they have suffered such terror, then why shouldn't anyone else or the entire world for that matter? Her gross malfeasance was vampiric, mad; it ran rampant as the great influenza. What made it worse was that she had charisma that lead others to attach to her like flies would syrup and though her manipulation and crude treatment gave no quarter, they remained as if afraid to leave her, as sheep during the spring slaughter, docility that defeated their natural reasoning of basic survival. It is a true wonder why the less evolved outlast us all. A cockroach can live a month without its head- the refusal to evolve has mysteriously become the way of survival. This especial fact, I suppose, escaped Darwin's notes. Lana as a woman was repugnant in the eyes of society- what made her seductive in my light was the fact that she was a firebreather, a survivor. She may have not survived in the social standard, but she did. A failure as a human being, she was a marvel and success in the bedroom. A woman is a woman, able to penetrate a man's armor of chivalry at any given shamelessness; a woman who can eradicate, emancipate and asphyxiate a man's high standards, is a shameless woman indeed. Lana had no sense of friendship, of devotion; she would offer you the illusion of devotion, leave you with such a belief and commit a one-night stand that very day. It would be highly erroneous to say that her manipulation was obsessive-compulsive, that would only imply that she had no control over such a desire; she was methodical- manipulation was her means of survival and survival was her virtue.

Sunset during a Thursday at Bennigans- there are protesters in the streets, picketers, deconstructionist and reformist, lobbying against war, against hunger caused by war. My drive is only for the life in their bodies, the beat of their feet against the pavement, the union of all, the antagonist and protagonist, by the breath that we share. There is poetry in all that we do. Philosophy falls to our step, into cadence, in tandem, we toast not to our beauty but the beauty of our attempts, to our defects, the defect is beauty because the defect is real, how much more can beauty be true? I text Amelia, who is overseas, a simple message to confess my thinking of her, put back another brew and called up Lana to see if she was in the vicinity. She wasn't, but with time, she says, she may be headed my way, to keep her a beer on ice. It was seven brews and a batch of fried mushrooms later until she appeared, wearing a pair of denim jeans that complimented her thighs, hips and her ass brilliantly, a thin tank to that gave away the presence of the color of her black bra. Her hair was tied high into a tight bun and she adorned a pair of shades to divert the blinding sun. I turned and offered her a fresh beer timed flawlessly by the attending bartender, laid a kiss on her cheek and let my hands run the length of the side of her torso. There was vagueness in the air, the type that broke the prelude of a great performance short and hurried itself into the climax of suspense. There were words, words spoken just to be spoken, spoken to open her like a flower, to prepare it for the petal pull that would ensue the moment we fled the bar and found privacy, any privacy. We end up in an alley, hidden in the grace of the night itself and the indifference and pour of the crowd determined to meet its destinations, wherever they may be. I press her back against the wall, kiss her roughly. She drops her purse to wrap her arms around me as my hands grabs a tight grip of her ass, then her breast. Now she has fallen deep into the illusion, the transcendence of pleasure. Dropping to her knees, we both toggle with my belt and zipper, till both are clear and she releases my swollen phallus from my boxers. She places me in her mouth in haste, as though starved for the flow that contains over thirty types of protein and her body demanded its very nourishment for proper function. Unable to take anymore, I pulled her up from her knees, she spits on my phallus before she stands, snatch low her jeans with an uncompromising force, her panties followed, hung around her knees. I bend her all the way over and force her to grab her ankles, took hold of the seemingly solid lead with wings and force it into her tearing venus. By the time I had begun to throw her off balance with my thrust, pedestrians had noticed our tryst but it matter not, the surcease is never a compromise with the woman who wants to be transformed into a whore during coitus. A whore has no boundaries and no boundaries resurrects the primitism of man and his savagery, the blatant and heinous tearing and lacerations, the infliction of staggering punishment while single-mindedly chasing the orgasm- and it en route, the pain, the torture, the mistreatment causes the whore's womb to flutter, take flight and explode. She cums kissing the wall, I cum with my teeth in her neck, her hair wrapped tightly in my hands, attempting to catch my breath and recuperate from the amount expelled to reach that ephemeral cloud of cum.

Beer has always held a harsh history of destroying my libido- I wanted her again but I had nothing to show for it. After about three minutes of her attempt to soothe my impotence, she pushes me off of her and calls me pathetic. The next day her minions and cronies were spectators at her regale and found an earnest humor in the belief that I was unable to perform. I once took umbrage under the false pretense of asexuality to wheedle my way into the bedroom of twins, all in the effort to rebound from such embarrassment. There is something about a man, embarrassment and rejection that we just can't handle; we'll climb Mount Everest, swim the English Channel to France, transverse Australia by foot just to redeem any disgrace that has stained our reputations. It is a born affliction in a man to do such things, to uphold his honor and remain gleaming in immaculate masculinity for the sake of self or the attention of a woman. The Rodentia is the prime façade of the perplexities of man. During mating season, the males would go on an expedition to find as many females as possible and impregnate them. This mating season goes on for weeks and in the midst of their clandestine procreation, everything else takes a backseat; they forget to eat, to drink and eventually they die. The male, despite the species, will aggrandize himself, be exalted at all cause, even if it means taking the last expedition that we will ever take, take what is essential and radically make it nugatory.

Someday fruit will bear, barest near us, nearest to what is dearest to us, leaving naked the composure that all writers truly write. The anatomy of our being, the volumes of poetry that details our lives, the discography burned into our minds, minds not our wants, but gives into our will, the will to go on, the will to live, the will to want. Vice is necessary and the adverse is only labeled the versus when in conflict with what is expected battling what is. So the sowing prevails as one can never truly give one's own biology that great struggle, that toggle to retain and maintain a bit of pride. Hannah sits on the bed, naked, throws her hair forward, it spills like a brunette waterfall as it brushes along the ground while she brushes through it- everything else she does is made of lie, are all lies. Erotic verses chant from my manuscript as she rises to dress, becomes a life of its own, a child who has been pulled from its uterine home into the world and takes it first breathe. She isn't thwarted a bit from our one night stand, our imprisonment in sobriety. A hippie who somehow was born much too late to have known Woodstock, Hannah believed in free love, expression and that our presence on this earth must be heavy and sure. And what better way to make our presence known than to make love, to engage in puppy love, the birds and the bees, the keeping of the paramour and cuckholds and enjoy the semen spray immediately following coitus interruptus. A Californian by heart, New Jersey-born, there was no taboo to Hannah but there were ways she refuted and refused to live. The hippies of the seventies and the beat-movers lack standards, lacked conformity and found only purity on the move, depending on people everywhere and giving up all their possessions to live a life outside of history, outside of measure and aegis. Hannah conformed to the non-conformers; she planned to not have a plan, rallied against West African chocolate slavers yet praised Chocolatiers. Love in itself carried a consistent altering definition from day to day in her eyes. She believed that it was a simple law of attraction, an undisputed pull of one's electricity to a source, if only she'd let me in, I would have proved to her that sexuality is much more complicated than it seemed. She was a feminist, not at heart, not due to belief or some crime committed against her person nor did she witness the suffrage or human affliction in which a woman endures and manage to feel a legitimate care; it was because she believed no man would have her. In response, she threw up a false façade courted with the belief that men are only creatures and consumers of physical beauty. She has aged much quicker than she had once phantom time to grasp the reign of youth. She was every man's dream over Facebook but in person she was diluted, schemish to establish rapport when a man spoke her name, a prudish decorum that negates the woman she tried to be. If she had any interest in her own drowning and self-destruction, perhaps then her views may possess a bit more substance but she only lied idle in the chance, in the possibility, that what she want and believed she deserved, may accidently fly into her as a pigeon into a pane-glass window. When a car crashes, people don't stop to see if anyone is okay, they want to see a dead body, they want something to pull them into a chaotic downfall, a reason to become the helpless victim. They seek a reason to run and update the session with their therapist that provides the palate of victimhood. We want to see the horror, the gore, crime and massacre printed on the front pages, dig into the crevice of every incident to exhume and catch a haze whiff off the affliction of infection. We drink vodka but we crave absinthe, we lick tragedy once and become gluttonous to its taste. We spend our days and nights in search of something or someone to devour whole, social and emotional cannibalism; we feed as parasites, not to nourish for the basic source, but to overwhelm, multiply and destroy. We have folded history so it is we who should attempt to iron out the wrinkles that are bluntly visible in our eyes and our demeanor.

There is fire in the sky, flowers in my heart as I roam the streets in search of a good meal. I am indecisive so I let the hunger be as an existentialist remains in a dark room without thinking to turn on the light switch. Osmotic shock strips the threads as I smile while thinking of nothing but the farrago of the nostalgia shops and boulevards I had yet to visit. Maya Deren's films sing in my mind as Piaf plays the streets near the subterraneans dwarfed by the Elways that rumble past, quaking the bridges and flats within a block's vicinity. The grace of the unknown neighborhood always reminds me of the fortune of friendship. Amelia's voice over the phone is a wonderful treat, a retreat to something I never had when I felt much obliged to appropriate. We cannot pinpoint when the soul erects to friendship or why it feels it must leave umbrage and stagger blindly into the pouring rain, but it does so in a brave and unquestionable manner, despite our prudence to opening ourselves to unknown character. We are all one and the same, on the thin line we are always near drifting or falling into the undesirable to the social structure- we are all demivierges who need but spread our legs to give our aperture over to deflowering.

A walk in the park, a short film shot on 8mm in an antique theatre, black and white skies, broken flocks of pigeons cluttering the sidewalks by the crowds. Clouds move in from Lake Michigan and hides the sun long enough for people to move from under the umbrella of trees in Grant Park, hug their friends, share a polish and coke and retreat the moment the burn returns. Women seek the passion of the day, of this life, of what may be. Possibilities are endless in the language shared between those seeking and struggling to weld human connection, to amalgamate a companionship. They sit on park benches and read Bronte, perfect their make-up in the mirrors while lunching, sip aperitifs in the windows where they can see the entire world roam by; everything else they do is lies, all lies.

I made my way to O'Hare airport, as I promised to see my mistress off. Mancha's two years in the states were great to her and she planned to return once she completed her doctorate. Though she and her retinue lived somewhat of a student's life those last two years, they departed first class, in the true style of dignitaries. I carried their bags, even fetched them a couple of ice mochas from the Starbucks in the terminal while they awaited boarding call. During the time with Mancha, I realized that I wasn't only sexually attracted to her nor did I only love her intellect, it was the fact that she was the descendant of an African monarchy that was never broken, whose bloodline was never cut. She represented the few of us Africans who never fell to slavery and that perhaps provided her with that perspective of believing that African-Americans were inferior, domesticated and molded to be pliable in that American way. When Moses led the Jews across the Red sea, her people were a tribe of Kings and Queens and for that, her history as my doctrine that I engraved into my being. Before departing, she asked that I adhere to my etiquette- knowing that I was a writer; she knew that our coexistence would inspire my talent somehow. It wasn't narcissism but her better judgment. The only thing she asked is that I use a nom-de-guerre in the place of her prestigious name and that I send her a copy of all my work highest priority. For that, I would be well rewarded and regarded in the highest of esteems. She knew that was truly no reason to distrust my promise, my obsequious nature- I had no interest in breaking our non-disclosure agreement; it would jeopardize her crown and the right to one day call herself a queen, a right which she dreamed of since the day she was born, anointed and held high amongst a proud tribal nation. Why not bury her indiscretion? She wasn't the only royalty enjoying the fruits of life outside of wedlock nor was she the first in the long line of monarchs before her. History should play itself out, not come to a sudden, crashing halt. I was one of perhaps a few men who'd had the privilege to lei with her. In her homeland, a man could be put to death for merely staring at her, so in my own way, I had laid down my life for her and in her own way, she recognized my sacrifice. In the days of slavery, a princess in captivity would kill herself rather sleep with a man that wasn't of great stature or chosen by her father. During colonialism, this reputation for the princess's sexual and social discrimination was legend and the very way that officers and diplomats of Europe confirmed greatness. They came from all over the world and spent nearly half a year worth of salary to take into their bed a princess, a woman who chose only the finest stock of men. Many of these men abandoned their wives and married princesses; others took them into harems as mistresses so that no other man could have them. I had nothing to give other than a curiosity, an attempt, the beauty of the attempt and by no small measure was it meager. The sum of one man's truth, one man's romance, however antiquated, will always separate him from the common man driven face to face with their own biology. Mancha's plane arrives. We exchange our last hugs, our last kisses, she boards her flight and I lose her, now along with Amelia, to the surrealism of Europe.

There were photographs taken, brews sipped, jokes to liven the friendship that glistered between us- the prelude of Leigh and Linotte. Triangles have fallen in the history of human interaction, the Bermuda triangle has even devoured the ideal of triangles, the epicenter of love and the nexus of pleasure coming full circle. There is a house filled with people, listeners, eaves-droppers and skeptics- we make plans to escape into town to the seclusion, comfort and freedom of a motel 6. A motel maintains the aura of forbidden, the retreat of the sisterhood of the night as they ply their trade to travelers as they pass through. It was the sleaziness, the gaudy and shabby that we craved the cheapness and authenticity.

We stop off along the way to purchase cases of brew, vodka for, Linotte's poison. She had brought a bag of goodies; a whip and a strobe light. Diet coke acts as the chaser for her vodka, as she orders a huge cup at the same corner store where Leigh purchases the brews. We had no plans to see the outside world until we all emerge back into it sore, taken back, in painful joy, drained of all the coital fluids that our body would be able to muster that night.

For weeks Linotte has been estranged from us. Messages between us all are of mutual need and want, our bodies begging for the encore performance that once took place on a Halloween night gone livid. Plans are devised between Leigh and I to again make her our whore, to make part of her regret ever walking through the door of that motel room. We draw room thirty, a small room on the lower level not far from the pool. No ice is in the room so Leigh and I walk in our socks with a bucket and emptied trashcans to collect as much needed to keep our brews cool throughout the entire ordeal. Filling the sink with ice, we stick the brews as deep as possible into the freeze and filled the trashcan with the remaining available.

Linotte's sexuality is legend- the very presence of her vouches such truth. Grabbing a small clear plastic cup, she finally gets the opportunity to take shots of her beloved spirit. We fill the cup to the top and hand her the task of finishing it all in a short manner, to binge herself into preparation, a prerequisite of what she'd need to get through the ravishing that would ensue. We play various music, Leigh cuts cocaine on the table next to the bed, very thins line, folds a Benjamin Franklin portrait in preparation for its trip up his nasal vault. I collect residue with my finger, clean clear tobacco from a cartwright, place it inside carefully, twist shut the top, hold it parallel and find a piece of fire to light it. The massive drag and slow exhale leaves me afloat, adrift, as all who seek to escape the presence, just to escape again. Leaning against the wall, I catch my balance as my equilibrium still swims in delirium, as Leigh and Linotte initiates puppy play that usually, inevitable falls into coitus. He partially pulls Linotte's pants and panties down, tastes her venus as I record the feature. I run my hands along her breast, still held by a pink bra that she favors that favors her beauty very brilliantly as she soaks in the sensation of Leigh's lips roaming her pendendulum. She lives there only temporarily, until she fights us off to continue drinking, not wanting to engage in what she knew could possibly be the worst death anyone could die while still living. We convince her to keep her pants and panties absent, only her bra still on- she complies as she does when she knows our insistence wouldn't wear thin. Leigh and I strip down to nothing and continue our mass devouring of brews and smoking cartwrights intermittingly, chatting, enjoying music and the time in our world.

Linotte attempts to excuse herself to the bathroom to make water, but privacy has long fallen away between us all. Leigh waits for Linotte to seat herself on the toilet, then places his hands between her legs, awaiting the fall of water. She is unable to perform, due to the very slightest touch to her flush button sends her into a rage of arousal. Leigh adjusts his hand away from her conillon and then water comes. It fills his hand a bit. When she has stopped making water, he licks his fingers clean and embraces Linotte for a deep, sensual kissed wrapped in taboo. All the while, I film, half erect, wondrous of the very experience. I find myself falling behind their evolution, their expression consistently. I spent year in repressing my post-trauma masochism and the very stage to express it, was now at hand and stage fright visited frequently.

We return back to the table, Linotte on Leigh's lap as we switch songs, songs for the moment, that implies sex, the very mood for our nights. Linotte's teasing carries an all-purpose high. She alone builds anticipation to sex, transcends sex and reintroduces it as it has never been presented thus far to anyone she chooses to worship, anyone she chooses to dominate. Again she and Leigh engage in puppy play as I record the dream unfolding. I place my phallus in her mouth as Leigh again visits her venus. Her lips, moistened by her make of saliva to allow it to go in and out of her mouth easily, runs along the shaft, followed by her tongue ring. She again comes to and resists our attempt to penetrate, rises from the bed and returns to her cup of vodka. I take it from her, dip my phallus into it and place it in her mouth, to aid her ingestion level.

Strobe lights are now going, giving us only minute milliseconds of visions and sights of each other. Our temperatures begin to rise and Linotte again, resists, then mentions she has to go and make water again. I had the camera to Leigh, sit Linotte on the toilet and again place my phallus in her mouth. When it is rod hard, I place one of my legs over her and one under, reaching my hardened phallus between her legs. She begins to make water all over it and it runs along my shaft, down my leg and onto the floor. Leigh feels the excitement of voyeurism, my excitement, grabs a hand full of urine from the floor and throws it all over us as we continue to intertwine. She reaches for my penis and sucks all of her water off, stands and we clean one another off.

Linotte has a game plan and that is to drive Leigh and I to the breaking point. She resists so much that we conspire to rape her, to take what is rightfully ours by force method. She pulls a whip and whips Leigh's phallus till red, then she performs the same method on me until she craves the lashes themselves on her flush button. Leigh gives her three lashes that send her over in pain and pleasure, she bites into my phallus alarmingly and I cringe in an overwhelming pain, which transforms into pleasure as it fades and I am again erect. She pulls for both of our phalluses, places them together and performs fellatio as we free her finally from her bra. She pulls away as we are both stiff and we both reach for a breast a piece and suck on her nipple rings, the sound of metal and suckling conflated. Her resistance again arises and we are nearly defeated as the brews pacify us a bit.

Feeling the ennui growing, spontaneously, Linotte splays herself on the bed, waiting to be taken, waiting what may come of our anticipation. Our lips and tongue explore everywhere on her. She implores me to remove a necklace from her neck- I attempt as she sucks on my phallus to a point where I am unable to do anything but sit in euphoria. Her body is flailing from Leigh's shoving fingers and rough cunnilingus yet her fellatio is unvarying. Leigh climbs up to place himself in her mouth as I rotate around him, grabs the back of both her thighs, spread her legs and push inside of her pink and nattering venus. To penetrate her is like no other penetration- her venus holds a memory cell, a conforming to the phallus that enters her repeatedly, the husband's knot devised by the gynecologist for the continuing pleasure. I fuck her relentlessly hard, her legs pressed over her torso, choking as Leigh shoves his phallus deep into her throat, scraping her frenulum, lodging between her tonsils. The sound of choking and the shafting of my phallus in and out of her venus prevail; moans find their way into the smattering. We twist her, we turn her, her body contorts, painfully- we are indifferent chasing the orgasm, chafing and tearing deep into her whipple-tickle. The sound of a broken woman is the sound of the heroic masochist; the pain, the pleasure, fatigue, the rawness and numbness, the begging to stop all mingles and our pleasure becomes punishment at once. If a woman isn't sore in every orifice when you are finished with her, then you aren't finished, there must be pain, capacity of the recovery, the gather of palettes and reunion of capillary tears. I pull from her and release two hot bolts of cum on her venus and anus as she swallows Leigh's seed. We fall off of her and we are deep into sleep with no hesitation.

I began to come out of my dreams in time to meet their awakening. Lying between us, Linotte reaches down and plays with my morning wood as I suck her breast, attempting to expel the lactation that her hormones have enabled. Leigh begins to fuck her tightly and hard from the back and I made my way up to place my phallus into her mouth, fucking it as I would her venus. She again visits the delirium of being penetrated by two men, her mouth and venus simultaneously at work. Her jaw is relaxed and I feel her tongue ring scraping the growing abrasion on the top of my shaft, just south of my second head. I climb into her venus once more as Leigh pulls her half way off the bed, while she hangs low; he shoves his phallus into her mouth upside down. She brags of her ability to deepthroat much more effectively that way. My morning wood has me flustered and I am deeply in her, hard and quick as she attempts to moan while Leigh is still down her throat. For the first time, I cum deep inside a woman, I press myself deeply into her as her cervix rattles and opens to accept the possible gestation of miscegenation. I pull away to see Leigh take her violently, they roll into a great ball of cum chasing and fall off the bed onto the floor. Linotte'skull bounces off the floor- I scurry over, not to rescue the damsel that prefers the distress, but as she is dizzy and mere concussed, I stick my phallus in her mouth as she instinctively suckles, unsure as of where she is and what had happened. Again an orgasm works its way through my urethra- I lay Linotte on the bed, splay her out, feel the peaks and valley of her cell. Within her first stage of sleep, she still felt my hands circumnavigate her flesh and she signified it with squirms and moans. I then cover her back with another shot of cum- it lies in the crevice of her spine and drips down the side of her torso. Her moan then at the feeling of warmth was a soft sigh, the identical that escaped her lips when she is first penetrated by a throbbing and erect phallus secreting and made solid by the honed skill of her blowjob. The human body is able to handle forty-five Del units of pain; a woman giving birth endures up to 57 Del units of pain, which is equivalent to twenty bones fracturing simultaneously in the body. Linotte has passed the child, she herself, a child still in this world in search of her paper womb, the likeness to the sooth she enjoyed in her uterine world, invites punishment, invites del units of all measure onto her and she fears not the level to which it may reach, all she fears is the absence of the pain, the del unit that is the threat far away.

Warm water falls over my body as the pain hits me from all the injuries I sustained only hours before. I crave the pain, the post trauma and I am the happiest man to ever have had his skin broken. I am dead to the outside world, found death in that very room. My phallus was swollen and a scab had grown where the Linotte's bite was set. The burning sensation of washing it grew and I continued to do it to get all of the sensations of being alive that I could out of it. Genius, mad genius then imbues paragraphs and sonnets become impregnable, contorted distortions glister with black canaries in flight. Eighteen years ago, the lash that achieved my first arousal still sits on my flesh and it is now accompanied by the lashes I crave. Much flesh has been sacrificed as much more will be, scars have calloused over as many shall- I hold such vice close and hope that when my walk is done, when all is said and done and this road that I've chosen not to take but the one I choose to continue down, that my place will not be given to the ones who have never lived due to the fear of living. "God is dead" said Zarathustra and the man who've always been too weak to imagine his own demise. The ingloriousness of compartmentalizing is glorious for that one who has turned inward to introspection, to not only see art, but to live it, to make it, to be it, to not only build a genre but become in itself, the genre.

We return in subtle and most comfortable conversation, hangovers hang over our heads like halos. Linotte's shades shield my eyes from the brightness of the sun as we emerge back into the world, the other world that we have consolidated to escape. If one can create a dream in this life, they can do it in the next- they can sleep dreamless sleep, wake and stroll slowly, without a clan destined speed but one that allows them to enjoy and appreciate the road along the way. Murders sing from up above as we drive, windows down, wind flowing through the car, pulling smoke from Leigh's cartwright, carrying Linotte's long hair into a hover. The sweetness of our doldrum radiates as the sun does in the highest of spring days- at that moment, I attempt to recall the last time we ventured out together in the daylight. The night was our haunt, the glue in which fragments we plastered together temporarily until they once again crave the chicotte, craved the sew of the seams that formed the cloak of utero.

Edgar Lee Master's once wrote:

"There is a quiet in my heart,

like one who rests from days of pain;

outside the sparrows in the roof

are chirping in the dripping rain."

Being alone is one of those things that can never get old- everyday, the reality of loneliness inflicts one with such an excruciating pain, a unique pain that touches the human frame and self-understanding is suddenly rekindled. It is a pain that is unable to be suppressed by the eyes and the mind manufactures dreams of conformity, of confidence, of companionship. One then, upon waking, is obliged to find the courage to live up to those dreams or perish slowly in that monotony of everyday slaughter, which is much easier than facing a world which has moved on and forgotten you. The eyes tell a story deeper than the soul can burrow. Art is pain, liberation, inspiration- the night sky is there for one to paint, for one to watch, for one to hope for the comets that have fallen long ago to return, replant themselves in the up-aboves, and fall once more. What prohibits the mind to wonder? To be seduced by the tricks of light? Or to roam beyond its theoretical self and bloom where the tulips might?

Driven back to the dark roads and nightfall of Brentwood, I am still a loyal believer of atonement, perhaps even a fanatic. I've been defeated by this world thus far and of that fact, I am not ashamed to join the legions who too are finding nothing but that ass end of humanity gone into teeth. It's not the flesh of a man that constitutes his demeanor; it's the man inside the flesh, the heart inside the incubating cell. There is no forfeited kindness or reduction of chaste born into anyone; we learn to hate, to conspire, to cynicism. And under no isolated consequence, all in all, we can also learn to love, learn to forgive without ill-will; such passivity is an integral part of our profound nature. The quiet in my heart is not an injustice brutally spelled on heroic nor heretic, the sparrows that chirp on the rooftops sing because their liberation is but a phantom, a frantic need to find oneself which painfully involves the frantic need to search. The casual search itself can rip through one like a blade and the paper that makes up our artificial uterine haven may just peel away and tear open to abruption. I don't belong to this world nor will I the next; my demise will go unnoticed, as my existence has, stone beneath the growing sand.

There is a quiet in my heart that seems to deplete any chance of hedonism. Despite how much a man accumulates materialistically, his life is incomplete without a legacy to leave behind, without someone to love or at times of insecurity, vilify; he diminishes with time. Men who are remembered in history are the fortunates in a long line of those who never had the courage or the strength to muster courage to stand out. If he is lucky- he may get a mention or two in the column of their town's obituary or become the topic of conversation among wonderer's with a lack of a better idea. Infamy grants a man at least a guaranteed few years of topic. Victory defines the base of man, in argument, with his significant other, even his grapple with self. A man is most alive during sex and when fighting a cause- yet he doesn't feel true adrenaline unless he pulls out victorious on flesh.

I've found a home, cold and damp, that sits on the contours of nightfall as a vagrom on the rails- one who sleeps in the worn holes of shambled trailers- mind is a worn hole, the askew and the transposed impasses to tunnels left abandoned, to songs fallen into the earth. I've loved to the point of insanity; insane is what many have labeled my love, which is as deep and dark as the gapes in the earth- where if one spends too much time, will too, find insanity.

www.ingramcontent.com/pod-product-compliance
Ingram Content Group UK Ltd.
Pitfield, Milton Keynes, MK11 3LW, UK
UKHW051135260726
13967UKWH00010B/3055

9 781304 733894